A Darker Shadow

By Jacqui Callen

Other stories by Jacqui Callen

With Terry Fowler

Penetrated by the Tentacle
(a gay tentacle love story)

Author's Note

Hello there. It's me again, Jacqui Callen, with something new for you to read.

First up, this is one of those stories that came to me while I was away from home in an uncomfortable space and moment in my life. The germ of the story invaded my nightmares one restless night and I just could not resist setting it down in words once I awakened.

This novel isn't a part of the *Alien Tentacle* series of stories. In fact, it's not even a tentacle novel.

This protagonist feeds on the life force of other living things. This is a story that will either be a stand-alone or if it has a good response from you, the reader, I may consider expanding it into its own series.

It's a different kind of story for me to write. It might not seem so at first, but as you read into it, you will see that I wanted to do something that put me into another area of my comfort zone. An area I had not really taken the time to explore.

I hope you enjoy reading it at least as much as I enjoyed writing it.

And I hope it freaks the living shit out of you.

Prologue

My story begins about fifty-five years ago, when I was in my late teens and feeling as though I could take on the world. For a woman in that time, I was considered a bit of a tomboy, and my parents had been unhappy that I had not gone the "acceptable" route and gone to college to find a man, marry him and then settle down to keep house and raise their grandkids on a home economics degree.

That's how things were done in those days. You didn't see female lawyers, doctors, or white collar businesswomen. To say they were few and few between would be a massive understatement.

I think they were concerned that a spinster daughter would be a burden on them, or at "worst" one of those pants-wearing, make-up shunning, "ladies in comfortable shoes" never spoken of in polite society of the day.

I had an aunt, one of my father's sisters, of whom no one ever spoke except in whispers. Agnes had lived with another spinster, a woman called Eileen, for the past couple decades. Eileen wrote and published poetry when she was not at her job waiting tables at a local coffee shop and Agnes worked in the ticket booth at the local movie theater.

Agnes had worked at an aircraft plant during the War, and had left her job kicking and screaming when the War had ended.

She had met Eileen one morning after the end of her shift, and they had started talking about this and that, and that finally became the start of their relationship.

My parents still preferred to call them "roommates" whenever the subject came up. Until I reached my eighteenth birthday, I had only seen Agnes and Eileen a few times, when I had managed to sneak out to meet them in the next town over, where they lived.

I remember that they were pretty cool ladies. Lots of fun. Agnes had once broached the subject of my sexuality when it became apparent, even to her, that I was not on the "boyfriend track". I had thanked her for her concern and told her that while I was glad that she was happy, I was an unrepentant heterosexual. Both she and Eileen had laughed, and that had been the end of that discussion.

As the only girl in a family of six children, I had been expected to be the one to care for my parents and grandparents into their old age, but I refused to kowtow to social expectations. Now my brothers' wives would and in some cases already did, openly resenting me for settling that future role on them.

I liked boys, but didn't feel a need to tie myself down to one, and anyways, had not found one whose company interested me. Most of the boys in my small town wanted the "traditional" kind of girl, and that just was not me. It usually didn't take very long before I decided that a guy just was not worth my time and went my merry way.

I was a sexual creature and would probably have participated in Masters' and Johnson's scandalous study if I had known about it. It would have been right up my alley, I think.

A DARKER SHADOW

I had given the boys I knew in my hometown a polite "no" at first, and then had been more firm the more they pushed it. Finally, I could no longer stand their pressure and went off on my own, moving to the big city, where a group of similarly minded girls got a three-bedroom apartment together. We went to beat bars and absorbed the bizarre poetry and music of that generation, all so full of ourselves and thinking that we were "hip" while the "straights" were seen as modern-day dinosaurs.

Teenagers can be annoying, but they rarely realize it at the time.

During that time, I waited tables at a couple coffee shops and also did some work as a cigarette girl to make ends meet. Sometimes, I had managed to get laid when I saw a particularly cool guy with whom I wanted to spend an evening, but those relationships never lasted. I was not looking for those kinds of encounters, and oftentimes, I had to put a guy in his place when he tried to force the issue.

My parents, of course, were shocked at what I was doing, and kept begging me to come back "home". They didn't and would not know about the one-night stands, but the sheer thought that I was hanging around places that had anything to do with alcohol and cigarettes were anathema to my parents' conservative Christian upbringing. My mother once asked if I was *dancing*, but I simply laughed her question off.

She said she would pray for my soul. She probably did, too.

Dad even went so far as to offer to build me a detached cottage next to the house for me to live in, if only I would leave the insanity of the city.

I, of course, declined his generous offer and he told me that God would punish me and I would regret my decision.

So what was it that finally happened?

I became a monster.

I had been made in an unmarked, abandoned mine. I really should have been paying better attention when I had started walking in the area, because I knew that some of the old gold miners had tried their luck in these hills.

I was on vacation in California after scrimping and saving a year's tips and wages. I had carefully planned my escape from the Midwest. I didn't even know if I was going to return. If I decided I liked it enough, I might stay. Waitressing jobs were not too hard to pick up if you had experience, so I was not worried about that.

In fact, a waitress I knew, Peggy, had an uncle who owned and ran a greasy spoon in Northern California. He had indicated that he would be willing to give me a chance if and when I decided to stop by. I figured that I might take on a job there temporarily, if only to make a bit more money to live on.

At that time, I was paying ten bucks a week to stay in a local boarding house, so my expenses were not too terrible, especially as what I was paid also included one hot meal a day. I was not a picky eater, so I was happy to eat whatever Mrs. Stinson put on the table in front of us, as long as I didn't have to cook it.

It was an idyllic time, and I spent most of my days out exploring the area, writing my own bad poetry and indulging the sense of wanderlust I had. I had taken an apple or a peach along as a snack, as well as a canteen full of water to drink.

I felt a freedom I had never had where I had grown up. It made me more willing to take chances. That willingness to take foolish chances is what probably what ultimately killed me as a human being.

One

I had been out hiking alone, and had stumbled into my fate when the roof of an old mine's thin ceiling had broken through. My terrified screams startled some squirrels up in the trees, and a few birds flew away, but other than that, there was nothing in the area to hear me, and nothing living to care that it had happened.

I fell quite a distance and had broken my ankle when I landed on the dirt far below. As this was long before the days of cell phones, my chances of escape were severely limited. I fully expected to meet my death in that hole. I remember wondering if Heaven existed and if I would get to go there after all.

Only the light of my flashlight I carried with me in the event of staying out after dark lit the area, but the battery was quickly going dead and soon I had been swallowed up in the darkness.

At first, I had thought the whispering I had heard was my imagination. It came from the part of the mine shaft that I could not see into. My initial thought that it was wind being forced through the curves and partial cave-ins along the tunnel were quashed when it dawned on me that I was not feeling any of that imaginary wind where I lay crippled on the ground.

The whispering seemed unhappy, somehow, as though it was lonely and somehow afraid as well. What could make something that be?

I called out, thinking that by some wild chance, another human might be trapped down there with me, but no answer came but the excited whispering from beyond my field of vision.

When the battery in my flashlight died several hours later, the whispering came even closer, and then the cold touch of the shadows began to crawl over my skin.

Terror and horror down to my very bones overtook me, tossing my formerly fearless nature to the wolves. The ranting of the preacher on Wednesdays and Sundays railed in the back of my mind and I was convinced that the Devil, himself, had come for me because of my disobedience and all my other sins. Heaven was to be denied me, and that fate was too much for me to bear.

I screamed, and when I did, it was as if the shadows streamed down into my mouth and my nose, choking me as they filled me up. I gasped from lack of breath, and the horrible feeling and uncontrollable shivering as the warmth of my body went away and the shadows made themselves at home within me.

I began convulsing as they wrought their changes within me. Bones cracked and shifted as they were reshaped to fit their new tasks, and various fluids and substances from within my body were forced out in a violent torrent during that time. I could not tell you how long it lasted, but to me, it seemed an eternity.

My screaming went on, but in time it became only a whisper. The same whisper that now would forever be my only way of speaking, but now I could understand what those shadows were saying. I didn't want to be able to understand them, their words were so horrible to consider.

The shadows were hungry, and they wanted me to climb out of the mine shaft and feed. It had been so very long since last they had fed, and their hunger made me feel as though I was indeed starving. What little energy they had been able to glean from me without killing me completely had enabled them to transform and turn me into their vessel.

During that transformation, my body had changed, and had purged itself completely. A massive amount of shit, urine, and vomit pooled on the ground around me, and I could not get away from it fast enough.

I didn't even stop to consider the fact that my leg no longer appeared to be broken and that I shed my clothing as quickly as I possibly could.

No, I dug my claws into the wall, scaling it like a lizard would have done, and the next thing I knew, I was standing at the top of the hole and was looking out at the black landscape.

The shadows whispered and laughed. They were free once more.

Desperate for something to eat, my nostrils flared and I smelled something big and warm not too terribly far away. Moving silently across the ground at a respectable speed, I found myself facing what appeared to be a lost cow. My hunger flared wildly and suddenly I was on it, my mouth clamped to its nose and inhaling while the cow fought to break free. It didn't occur to me to realize that I didn't have to exhale or that I was not actually breathing any longer.

My claws dug into the creature's hide, securing my hold there, and the time finally came when the cow was weakened to the point of collapse. My changed aspect allowed me to simply remain where I was as I continued to drink down the life of the unfortunate cow. Eventually I had to stop, as the cow had been reduced to a pile of black dust.

Only then, the shadows' gluttonous hunger sated, was I able to take a look at myself in the moonlight.

Impossibly black elongated fingers and toes ended in sharp, curved talons. This was not a black such as one might see with a person of African ancestry. This was the black of the shadows at the very back of an old granny's closet in a very old and creaky house.

My breasts, once fairly ample, were almost no longer there. My nipples had been eliminated entirely. In fact, my body looked very little like what it once had. My abdomen was pulled in to the point that I could see the outline of my lowest ribs through the scales that were now my skin. My hips looked boney, as did my knees and elbows.

Examining myself further, I found that I had no openings in my lower torso. Small, tight buttocks, but no rectum. I also no longer had a vagina between my legs. For some reason unknown to me, my clitoris remained and was still at least as sensitive as it had been while I was still human. It tingled as my questing fingers touched it, and an almost electric shock went through me as one of my claws caught on its hood.

Not painful. Sexual. I cried out in what could only be described as the sound of lust.

A surge of desire shot through me at the sensation, and I worried at the little hard knob even more until my knees felt weak. Falling to them, I continued to pleasure myself, consumed with that hot, throbbing need. I could not stop myself from rubbing my clit until my orgasm exploded out of me in a whispered shriek of release.

The shadows giggled. I should be happy that they'd let me keep that bit, they told me. How kind of them.

A DARKER SHADOW

I looked like a bizarre caricature of a human being now, albeit in jet black. Feeling my face, it seemed as though its shape was pretty much the same, except now with sharper cheekbones. My ears were slightly higher on each side of my head now, turning in response to sounds and each coming to a sharp point.

Something, however, had happened with my mouth and jaw, and they were able to open much further than they had while I was still human. It would allow me to engulf nearly any nose or mouth in order to feed successfully.

The shadows had fed upon every last bit of the fat of my formerly human body as they worked and left me as pure skin, muscle and bone. Later I found that I could stand in one place for hours on end, provided that I was not in danger of being placed in the light during that time. At least once, I had been mistaken for some kind of bizarre statue. Think something along the lines of H.R. Giger, whose work I saw on a movie poster a few decades ago, and you would get an idea of my new appearance.

It didn't take me long to learn that my existence was no longer my own. My terrible masters held my obedience in their insubstantial hands, and I had no choice but to do their bidding, no matter how horrible it might be.

Two

I was hungry, so very hungry, but for now, I was trapped until the lights went away. The light would burn me if I left the cool, comfortable shadows that now graciously sheltered me. It took a long time for those burns to heal, and I didn't want to be crippled while I was hunting.

An incautious rat had provided a small snack as I waited, but something that small didn't hold enough life energy for me to live on. I needed at least a medium sized dog if I was going to keep from losing my mind completely. I found that I was wringing my hands in nervous anticipation, my long curved claws clicking softly against one another as they touched.

I had been an idiot to shelter in a construction zone. This one night, the crew had not turned off their lighting, and I had been trapped in the glare of the single low-wattage bulb that hung overhead.

Yes, you heard that right. A single bulb's light was enough to drive me back into the soothing darkness. My jet black skin could not tolerate even that much light. I had learned that quite painfully in the very beginning. The beam of a flashlight in simply passing over my skin, had caused it to bubble like tar, leaving a raw black wound behind that burned as though I had lain in the middle of a blazing fire.

You only have to be taught that lesson once before learning it all too well.

Moonlight didn't harm me. Something about it was different from any other light source. Maybe it was because moonlight is reflected sunlight, but the shadows have never told me, if they even know why.

I had not been slender, but I had not been fat, either, while I was still human. Now, I was overly slender, which the blackness of my skin only heightened. All of me was black, from my skin to my sharp teeth, to my flesh and my eyes. There was not a single jot of anything that a reasonable person would consider to be "color" on me. I presumed it was designed to make creatures like me able to hide better in the darkness. My skin was dull, rather than shiny, so they didn't reflect the light.

I was a creature of the shadows. Perhaps that was why the light of the sun and electrical light burned me so much.

It only seemed logical that such creatures would have thrived in the days before electricity and constant ambient light, but I had never met another like myself in the five years since this life of mine began.

I sat up a little as I heard activity going on somewhere near me. My ears caught the sound of something, someone, making his way down to where I hid. I sniffed the air and smelled a human, and unconsciously licked my lips in anticipation of the feast to come. I shifted my position to a crouch and waited for him to approach.

He was not long in coming. Soon, I saw what appeared to be a grimy homeless man with a filthy rag in his hands. It seemed as though he had designs on the light bulb that burned overhead.

All the better for me. Once it was gone, I would be free once more. I smiled, knowing he would never see me do it.

He stood underneath the flickering bulb, considering and muttering to himself. It appeared that he really wanted that light bulb. Pulling a couple broken cinderblocks over beneath the light fixture, he climbed atop them and used the rag to unscrew the bulb, plunging the room into blessed darkness.

I waited until he had reached the ground again before I struck, all four sets of claws snagging his heavy overcoat as I did so.

He never even had the chance to scream before I put my mouth to his and began to drink down the energy of his body and the terror that emerged from him in waves. When he tried to fight back, I clung to him like a leech, never breaking contact with his mouth. A midnight succubus draining his life away.

The energy fed me, while the terror caused my erect clitoris to begin throbbing with the desire that grew in me. I was a demonic dominatrix, getting off on the terror of my victims.

I wanted more and knew that this single human's energy would not, would never, be enough to satisfy me. It was always the same story for me that way.

As I continued to drain his life essence, his body began to collapse in upon itself, beginning with his extremities. When I finished my task, only a pile of dust remained on the ground, in the rough shape of a human being.

I dropped my hand to my crotch and finished myself off, my scream of triumph no more than a whisper, but the shadows were happy now. They had finally been fed. My cravings, however, had not been silenced.

The only evidence I ever left behind after a complete feeding was a pile of dust as black as I was. Looking at it, I swept a hand through the dust and stopped for a moment to regard the novelty of the outline of my hand on the cement slab. It looked as though someone had dragged their fingers through a pile of ashes and then attempted to wipe them off on the ground. After staring at the mark of my fingers a moment longer, I smeared the larger pile of dust over onto it to wipe it out of existence and then climbed out of my former prison.

You may have already figured out that I had excellent vision, even in pitch-blackness. I was the best of boogey-men, I suppose. I could hide in your closet or under your bed, as long as no one turned on a light or left a flashlight beneath it. In fact, I had hidden under a few beds over the years, when there was nowhere else I could hide when the dawn came once more.

I had removed more than a few batteries from their flashlights when I had been fortunate enough to find them unattended. Why give my victims a better chance of escaping my need? My hunger?

Before you ask, no, I don't wear any clothing unless I absolutely cannot avoid it. It feels more than a little unnatural against my skin and I cannot abide it for any length of time. Whatever it is that I am prefers to exist *au naturel*, as it were. I have never found another of my kind to find out what that might be.

That does not mean that I don't ever wear it, but if you were to see me, there is very little chance that it would be during the daylight hours. The light during that time of day is so intense that most clothing is completely ineffectual at keeping me safe.

Something else I learned the hard way.

A DARKER SHADOW

What do I look like? I will try and help you visualize my appearance.

As I have already said, I am jet black from head to toe, inside and out. I have claws on my fingers and toes which enable me to hang from some rather precarious walls and roofs or ceilings. When I moved, I tended to do so on all fours, rather than upright. I am not sure why that was, but it appeared to be my most "natural" posture. I was also much more limber than I had been as a human being. Almost disturbingly so.

I don't have much of a voice. It's more of a whisper than anything else, as though the shadows that made me took that as well, leaving me with a bare shadow of what my voice once had been. It is not a pretty or feminine sound, either, but something more neutral than anything else, but it can be rather sibilant when I use "s" sounds. No matter how I have worked to stop that, it's never worked, so I fancy that I must sound like some kind of ghostly snake when I speak.

I don't speak very often anyway. There is really no need. My conversations with my Masters were on a purely telepathic level.

I was glad that the light bulb was unscrewed, and I had taken a moment to crush it beneath my heel as I left my former prison behind.

Oh, did I forget to mention that I am covered in something that resembles very hard scales? The glass didn't prick me even slightly as I ground it into dust beneath my heel. I had come to hate the light, even as I missed it. No one said that things had to make sense, did they? No, they didn't.

I was too close to the edge of town, and the ambient light was starting to make me uncomfortable. Urban sprawl was not good, as far as I was concerned. It made it even more difficult for me to do what I needed to do in order to live. When I had first been made, there had been much less development, so I had an easier time moving between one place and another, but with the encroachment of humanity into those wild places, their accursed artificial light had come with them.

So you are asking why I have not killed myself, since I hate what I am. That is a reasonable question, and I will tell you.

I was born and raised in a deeply religious household, and it was drummed into me from the time I was a child able to understand the concept that suicide is a sin that will land your soul in hell. I valued my soul, whatever that was anymore, so offing myself just was not in the cards for me. Also, I don't believe my Masters would allow me to end myself. I am their creature, and I must obey their demands. The one time I had screwed up the courage to try to end myself, my masters had taken control of my mind and had not released their absolute control until I had thoroughly repented of my temerity.

I took lives to survive. I tried to feed only from animals, but I was not always that lucky when I got hungry, and when that happened, I was not always in control of myself. If I came across a human, then the human became my meal if there was no alternative.

When I fed, I fed from whatever life energy they possessed. I drink it down like a thirsty man gulps water, but what I took from living things was not tangible. It was the energy, the electricity, perhaps, of a living creature.

It would not be long before dawn came. I could feel it approach, and knew I had to find a dark enough shelter for myself and which had little chance of turning into another prison.

A DARKER SHADOW

Running along in the odd four-legged lope I used when I had to move quickly, I searched for something appropriate, but it seemed as though most places I found would soon be illuminated by the light of day. A nearby wildlife park seemed to be the best location to look, so that was where I went.

After much searching and dismissal of several possibilities, I found a largish boulder and proceeded to dig a hole beneath it. The hole didn't need to be large, just big enough for me to pull my body in and make sure that the light would not touch me at all while I rested.

The top of the sun had just reached the horizon when I jammed myself into the hole I had just created. I swept some of the dirt I had dug out back toward the hole to try to keep as much light as possible away from me.

Then I slept.

"I think there is something in here," I heard a male voice from right next to where I hid, awakening me long before I was ready to do so. I tensed, but remained silent. With luck, the humans would leave and never know I was there. "C'mere, Tad."

The light padding sound of paws met my ears as what must have been the human's dog approached. Shortly, I heard rustling, and surmised that the human was pulling something out of a pack.

Whoever it was abruptly began to dig at the front of my hole, and I desperately tried to push myself further back into the cool shadow of the boulder behind me. The scraping sound became louder and I began to panic.

"Leave me!" I whispered at whoever was out there. "Leave me alone!"

The scraping sound stopped.

"What? There is a person in there!" Came the human's startled voice from outside. "Come on out of there, I am not going to hurt you."

Maybe I could stay silent and he would leave. I was not in a position to climb out and run. It was still daylight outside. The last thing I needed was a good Samaritan trying to help me.

A whine told me that there was a dog with the human, so he might not have another human with him. That made things a little easier for me, but not much. My hunger rose in me, and I fought to keep control of myself. This was not the time to make a mistake.

"Hey! Are you okay," he called into the hole. I knew he was trying to see me, but my sheer blackness kept him from separating me out from the shadows under the boulder. "Do you need me to call an ambulance?"

"I am fine," I whispered back at him. "Go away."

"I can't see how you are fine," he replied. "There is not much room in there at all."

"You need to leave," I responded, putting as much of my will into it as possible. "Take this gift of your life and go."

"Gift of my life? What the hell is that supposed to mean?" He sounded as though he felt a bit offended at my words. Suddenly, he was digging again, and I could not push myself any further back into the shadows.

I gave a scream as the light touched my knee. It was whisper-thin, but still high pitched and filled with the agony I felt. The human stopped digging. The sound I had made fitted nowhere in the human spectrum.

"What the hell?" he demanded. "What are you?"

I saw his face. He was dark haired and dark eyed, with strong features. I heard the growl of his dog as it recognized that I was not safe to be around. I was not particularly surprised when it forced its head between its master's and where I lay. It showed me its teeth, but didn't move to attack. Smarter than his master, by far.

"Tad, get back!" the human yelled at his dog, and pulled him out of the way.

That was surprising, and not a normal human response to a dog's growling. I keened a little as the agony from the burn on my knee throbbed.

The human reached out a hand and touched just below the burn, delicately sussing out my differences with his fingertips. I was surprised that he had not yet either jabbed violently at me with his shovel or started running for his life.

"What are you?" he asked again. I thought about it. "I have never seen anything like you in my life."

"I used to be like you," I told him in my sibilant whisper. "But not in a long time."

"You used to be *human*," I could hear the doubt in his voice. "Really. While you might be shaped a bit like one, you don't look or sound as though you were ever a human being."

"Yes, once," I replied. "No more."

The human still didn't leave. He was a stubborn one.

"I was made by the shadows," I told him. "I am dangerous. Very dangerous."

"How could you have been made by shadows," he asked me. "That doesn't make any sense."

"You can ask them that sometime," I retorted. "You might get an answer before they kill you."

The human was quiet for a moment before he spoke again.

"They didn't kill *you*," he pointed out. "You seem to be alive now."

I laughed, an ugly sound when rendered as a whisper.

"Don't make the mistake of thinking I am alive," I told him. "I have not been human for longer than you have been alive. I don't even breathe anymore."

"Then how can you talk? You need air to speak," he replied. What was he? A science major flaunting his degree? Go away, human!

"Whatever I am, it doesn't work according to human physics," I said. "You should already be running by now. The longer you wait, the more dangerous it will be for you."

"You don't seem very dangerous right now," he responded. "You won't even come out of that hole."

"I eat...living things," I told him. I didn't get into specifics. "I exist in the shadows."

"I eat living things," he replied. "I am a carnivore."

"I don't eat them that way," I said. "I have to eat them while they are still alive."

Why the hell was I being so open with him? It made no sense to me. Then I remembered that the masters were always listening and I became afraid.

That last bit got him. I could smell the smallest amount of fear as it started to break through his stubbornness. I knew he would understand what I implied, and maybe now realized the danger he was in from me.

"Your life sounds lonely," he stated.

"Life? What is life?" I asked bluntly. "I exist alone."

A DARKER SHADOW

He straightened suddenly and looked as though he might have decided to run. When he did, I would take my chances and run to find another den, although I knew I would pay for it with severe burns. I had had to do it in the past, and had hoped I would never have to do it again.

Life is full of these little disappointments.

If I was lucky, I would find somewhere deep and dark, where I could spend the next few weeks healing up again.

Surprisingly, he leaned forward again, reaching his hand in and touching mine, curling a finger around one of my own. I had not had a touch like that in longer than I could remember.

"I am sorry that I hurt you," he said, his voice strangely gentle. "I will push the dirt back in and leave you alone."

I was gobsmacked. Where the hell had that altruism come from? This was something from far out of my realm of experience. The humans simply didn't act this way when confronted with the likes of me.

Some of them still searched for me, wanting to capture and then study me. I killed any and all who came at me with that intention. Mercy on one of those was a lost cause.

It was not as though there would be anything left behind but that pile of black dust.

"Thank you," I replied automatically. Abruptly, the dirt that had been previously pulled away being pushed back in place and tamped down.

"Goodbye, whatever you are," he told me, and then I heard him start walking away.

"I am Bridget!" I called back at him.

Now why the fuck had I told him that? Well, he was far enough away, he might not have heard me.

"Goodbye, Bridget," he called back at me. "I am Donovan Thomas!"

Three

I halfway expected him to return armed and ready to deal with whatever I was, but that didn't happen.

Why had not I taken the opportunity to kill him when he had his hand in mine? I could easily have dragged him in and ended his life in but a moment with a slash of my claws or fangs, but I had not. I had let him leave unharmed and even gone so far as to share my name with him.

Was I finally going mad?

When nightfall came, I scrambled out of that hole as fast as I could and made my way into the forest, where I managed to feed from a doe that never saw me coming. The damage I took from her hooves healed almost as quickly as it happened, but that was not the case with wounds caused by the light. It was a completely different kind of animal, as far as healing was concerned.

The burn on my knee throbbed, and I knew it would be at least a week before it healed over enough that the sting would be gone. It would not scar, which still surprised me, but it would be there long enough for me to remember it.

I didn't stop running until I was far enough away that I thought he could not easily find me again.

I located an abandoned mine about ten miles from where I had encountered the human and nested in there for a time. It was unstable enough that the humans would not go in there without a particularly good reason, but I was not human, and could make a good lair out of just about anything that was cool and dark.

Old mines such as these were a welcome haven against the light of day and the chaos of the world. I had easily escaped collapses during stays in some of the most unstable mines in the world. It seemed as though the shadows were not willing to let me go.

The resident shadows welcomed me and wrapped themselves around me like relatives who had not seen me in ages. Their cool touch, once repulsive, was something my body enjoyed and craved. Perhaps they used such opportunities to communicate with one another. I was not privy to such knowledge.

I was merely their vessel. They shared with me only what they wished me to know. To them, I was simply a particularly smart dog. Sit. Stay. Feed.

Good doggie.

With the shadows offering suggestions and supervising, I scraped a ledge out the side of a wall and hid in there. I had designed it so that even with flashlights, a human would really have to work to make light shine into my nest.

The shadows liked my new home. I could hear them singing their merry song of death. They were never far from me. They were a part of me.

As it was, I was surprised when I heard a familiar voice coming from the outside of the cave a few hours later, accompanied by the sound of a wildly barking dog. I felt momentary terror of my own when I heard my name being said in connection with the shine of a flashlight.

Then the light suddenly went out.

"Bridget? Are you in there, Bridget?"

It was the human again. Why had not he been smart and just gone away and thanked God that I had left him alive?

The shadows whispered at me. *Who was this human, and why was he here? Invite him in,* they suggested. I could hear the hunger...and something else I could not identify...in their faint voices.

"Stay away from the shadows in here," I raised my voice as far as it could go. "The shadows are interested in you."

"Oh," he said, sounding a bit startled. "Can you come out of there?"

Not knowing why, I did, I did as I was bid and emerged from the mine's opening. The moon's light was enough for him to see what I looked like. He seemed a bit startled, but the fear I sensed in him was not as strong as I would have anticipated.

"So that is what you look like," he said. "It was hard to tell much of anything earlier today."

"Is that why you've come," I demanded. "To see what I looked like?"

The human appeared flustered and shook his head.

"You just sounded as though you needed a friend," he replied. "Thought you might want to have someone willing to sit and listen."

I heard a sound behind me, suddenly realized what was in the wind and didn't even have time to shout out a warning. As it was completely unlike anything I had ever known them to do, I was taken entirely by surprise.

Ah, a new servant to mold to our needs! You have done well, Bridget. They never used my name, and to hear them use it made me die a little inside. *Good doggie.*

The shadows boiled out from the cave and engulfed Donovan Thomas. As I had so very long ago, Donovan screamed out his terror and tried ineffectually to fight them off. I heard him begin to choke as they invaded his body and began their deadly work.

The dog, ignored by the shadows, let out a terrified yelp and ran away. I hoped it would stay away.

I begged the shadows to leave Donovan alone and let him go, but they would not listen. They had heard what had been said, took their opportunity and ran with it.

Two is better than one, they replied happily. *Foolish to waste an opportunity.*

I watched helplessly as Donovan vomited and shat himself, convulsing violently enough to break bones that were already breaking and reshaping themselves. He continued to vomit until nothing more could be forced from his mouth, and he shat until even undigested food no longer emerged from his guts.

He was empty and the refashioning of whatever internal organs he possessed could begin. As far as I could tell, the vast majority of mine were gone, so I suspected the same was being done to Donovan. It was not as if he would need them anymore in his changed aspect.

I tried to turn away, but the shadows would have none of it. One sent out a tentacle that slapped me across the face and cut me, despite its misty appearance. I knew better than to touch the wound and trusted that it would eventually heal.

Stay and watch, they ordered. *If you turn away, you will soon remember what it was like the last time you disobeyed us.*

Sickened by what I saw but forbidden to avert my eyes, I watched an odd murky-looking glow surround Donovan's body as the shadows began greedily to consume his body's fat, which his human body would have otherwise used as a source of energy in lean times.

Keeping us lean kept us hungry and obedient to our masters.

Once they had gorged themselves on the energy Donovan's body fat contained, it began to thin dramatically and his skin began to darken and become scaly like mine. The hair fell from his head as it had from mine decades earlier, scattering as he flailed wildly. His human teeth fell out upon the ground to be replaced by teeth better fitting a monster.

His mouth gaped open, and I saw as things *changed*, and it suddenly gaped even wider than it had before. His teeth looked like something out of a nightmare, and I abruptly knew I looked much the same.

Donovan screamed in agony as his ears dragged themselves up the sides of his head. I didn't remember when it had happened to me, I only knew that it had when I examined myself. He clapped his long black fingers to his ears as though he could force them to remain where they had been, but they continued their inexorable move upward. They broadened, changed, and then were just like mine.

I wondered if the shadows were dragging it out in order to play with him and drag out the pleasure they gained from causing terror. I would not have put it past them at all. I know they enjoyed the terror they instilled in me. They never seemed to tire of it.

His dark eyes became even darker, and then resolved into black orbs behind black lids. His fingers elongated by an additional knuckle, and the funny-looking toe shoes he'd been wearing tore open at the tips to reveal newly clawed toes.

I cried out in despair. My act of kindness being rewarded with this horror. His human screams eventually dwindled in volume to a whispered parody of terror, and not for the first time, I wished I could run as fast and far away as I was able.

But my masters would never permit me to do that. They had already ordered me to watch and told me what would happen if I defied them.

Several long minutes later, he no longer looked like the Donovan Thomas I had met only a few hours earlier. Instead, he looked like me. No longer human and now laying in a loose fetal position on the ground.

He was naked, having removed his filthy clothing and throwing it away as far as he could. With his clothing gone, I could see that the shadows had worked their same transformation on him as they had with me.

I saw what had once been his penis, but his testicles were gone. For some reason, they had brought his foreskin up and attached it to his groin, so that it was concealed much as a dog's would be.

It seemed a kind of veiled insult, removing that much more of his humanity. A reminder that they thought of us as little more than animals to do their bidding.

His eyes were wide and still held their terror. Somehow, I could see it in his black on black eyes. I could feel it and wanted to soothe his fears away.

I put out a hand to touch him and he flinched.

My heart, whatever it might resemble now, felt a sudden stab of agony at his rejection of my overtures. Less than twenty-four hours after finding me under that boulder, and he was getting a far greater explanation of what I was than he ever could have anticipated.

"I didn't know they would do that," I said to him. "If I had known, I had have done something to send you away to keep it from happening."

"What the fuck have you done," he asked me, black tears running from his eyes. "What have you done!"

"I have not done anything, Donovan," I replied. "I told you to stay away, but you would not listen to me."

"Make them change me back," he moaned. "I don't want to be this way."

"I can't do anything about it, Donovan," I wept black tears of my own. "If I could, I would have had them do the same to me a very long time ago."

He put a hand to his groin and pushed at the sheath that surrounded his penis. The organ in question jumped at his touch and he jerked his hand away as though it had burned him.

"Why?"

"I don't know," I said. "They're cruel masters."

"Masters? Are we their pets?"

"Listen to them laugh, Donovan," I told him. "They think what they have done is funny."

Donovan tried to scream in rage, but only his whispered rage emerged. He beat the ground with his hands and kept screaming.

The shadows were laughing.

We told you that you needed to behave. You should have eaten him when you met him, or at the least have killed him. Now we've made him like you. So much for your sympathy.

They said it to us both. Donovan heard what his fate *should* have been, as far as the shadows were concerned.

I screamed, too. It was not necessary for them to have done that to him, and to have mentally brutalized him even beyond that bothered me even more.

We are *kind*, they told me. *We didn't force you to kill him. You know very well that we could have done just that. He should be thanking us for our many kindnesses.*

Because of what we've done to you, you will exist forever, provided you don't do anything stupid and get yourself ended.

The shadows left us alone, returning to the cool safety of the mineshaft. They had had their fun for the night and now I had someone I had to teach, unless he decided he wanted to end himself.

"Kind?" he croaked. "How is what they have done to me kind?"

I understood his question but he still didn't comprehend what could have happened. It was time to show him. He had to be hungry. I know I had been, right after it had been done to me.

"Come with me, Donovan," I told him, taking his hand in mine. This time, he didn't pull away.

It felt odd. I had never held the hand of someone like me before. I found that I liked it, but kept that as much to myself as possible. I was not sure if the shadows were listening or not.

He rose and followed me into the forest that surrounded us. It was not too long before we found an area where several deer nested. I knew that I was hungry, and when I looked at him, I saw hunger reflected in his stance.

I gave him a gentle shove at the nest. The deer were unaware of our presence. At the same time, I picked my target and leaped in to grab it.

Giving an odd little cry of despair, Donovan leaped alongside me and grabbed the buck. After only a moment, he knew what he had to do and closed his mouth over the buck's nose and mouth. With that, he began to inhale the buck's energy

With the exception of my own prey, the rest of the herd scattered, probably hoping we would not be coming after them as well.

I fed from the yearling buck I had taken down while keeping an eye on Donovan. It was not long before his buck was reduced to dust and he stood there, staring down at the faint evidence that had already begun to blow away in the gentle breeze. Not long after, the remains of mine were doing the same.

I knew that I was aroused, as I always was after feeding, and judging by the presentation of Donovan's penis, knew he was as well.

Going to my knees, I gently pushed the sheath down and ran my tongue over its tip. The sheath was amazingly flexible and gathered down at the base of his penis like socks that had not been pulled up.

Donovan shuddered in response to the attention I was giving his member. I shuddered as well, as I had not had sexual contact like this in over fifty years. There was almost nothing that would make me step away now.

I moved my mouth over his dick, taking it all in, and began to suck, which made Donovan moan with pleasure. He looked down at me, wonder on his face.

In another moment, he was on the ground beside me, his fingers already down at my clitoris. After a quick investigation, he found that I was in a similar situation to his own and put his efforts into stimulating my clit. We were now both flexible enough that anything depicted in the Kama Sutra would have been easily accomplished.

Soon, we were in a sixty-nine position, and he tickled my clit with his tongue while I sucked and licked at his dick. Surprisingly, we came at the same time, screaming our release out as a whisper in the darkness.

Neither of us produced fluid, but the orgasms we had were just as real as one that humans would have. We shook and grimaced as our releases took us and left us spent on the flattened grass of the former deer nest.

Something told me they would not be back anytime soon. I sat up and looked over at Donovan, careful not to touch him. I didn't know what he might now be thinking.

Looking down at Donovan's penis, I could see that the sheath had already slid back over to cover its tip. His arousal seemed to have some effect on its ability to stay down and once he'd gotten his release, it went back up again.

"Oh my God, what have I done? I destroyed that poor deer!"

"That is what you are going to have to do in order to survive," I told him. "I tried to tell you to stay away. The shadows said that changing you is their version of being kind. They could just as easily have forced me to kill you."

Donovan looked at me, I knew that if his eyes had still been human, I would have seen disbelief reflected in them. As it was, I read it in his stance as he stared into my eyes.

"Do I look like you?" He asked me in a very small voice. "Are my eyes all black like yours are?"

I nodded.

"You are the essence of shadow," I said to him. "When you need to eat you will. It will come naturally to you. Don't try to fight it, it will only end badly."

"What's that supposed to mean?"

"We have a reasonable amount of autonomy," I said. "But if we don't feed, we start getting hungry, the shadows will force the issue. I don't think they necessarily stay with us, but they retain enough control that they know what we're doing."

"That doesn't make sense Bridget," Donovan protested. "How can they know what we're doing or not doing if they're far away?"

"You are never completely free of them," I explained. "We are their creatures, and we must do as they bid. In most cases, I have acted as a courier of sorts."

"That doesn't make sense," he said.

"At times, I have carried the shadows between one place and another. I have not had to do that a lot, but has happened. It's something you want to prepare yourself for."

"What does that mean?"

"They don't ride outside you," I told him quietly. "They enter you so they can travel from one place to another from within your body."

I think that if he had been able, Donovan would have started vomiting at that news. I know just thinking about it made me nauseous, and I no longer possessed anything resembling a stomach.

The shadows had told me that.

"Inside?" It was hard determining what Donovan was thinking just by looking at his face. I have never had to learn what our species facial expressions look like, and now I had to. "What do you mean *inside*?"

"You open your mouth and they flow inside."

"What if I refuse to open my mouth?"

"You really don't want to know what happens when you disobey," I put a hand on his leg. "You really don't. Please just do as they tell you."

His mouth worked and he bit his lower lip.

"Have you tried to disobey them?" I nodded.

"I have, but only a couple times. I learned my lesson very quickly." I tried to keep the sickness from my face.

"What did they do to you?"

"I spent some time looking like a large black worm," I told him, and then the dry heaves began. It took several minutes before I could regain control of myself. The overwhelming nausea at the memory of my time crawling over the ground mewling like a lost soul had trained me very well and never wanting to displease my masters again.

"A worm?"

"You don't understand," I told him. "I didn't have a proper mouth. I was unable to feed. I could barely move as I had no limbs. I could barely speak, and the sounds I made were as pathetic as the worm I was. They left me that way for weeks."

I shuddered and began to cry at the memory of how I had starved to the point where I had nearly descended into madness. I had not thought about that time in probably twenty years. Now, in an effort to keep Donovan from suffering a similar fate, I had to relive the horror. Somewhere, I knew the shadows were laughing.

"They can do that?" He asked. "How can make changes like that?"

"They only make us in this form because they want to," I told him. "They can make us look however they wish. I have not always been in this shape. The worm they seem to keep for punishment, but I have been in shapes that were far more horrific than this one that you see now. They didn't have to do what they did to you. I think it's a veiled reference to your dog."

"My dog?"

"I think they would have liked to force you to eat your dog as your first feeding, show you how powerful they are. However, your dog ran away faster than they could get to it, so hopefully he'll stay safe."

"Do they change animals to do what they want?"

"From what I can tell they consider non-human animals to not be intelligent enough to do what they wish. They simply consume them," I explained.

"How do they consume them?" Donovan asked me. "How do they feed?"

"We eat for them," I told him. "Sometimes, when you come back from feeding, they will cover you like a blanket, from head to toe. Once you open your mouth, they will slip inside of you emptying you of the energy that you've collected. They especially seem to like the terror you create when you feed, because that terror feeds you as well."

"I would think they would just give themselves a form with which they could feed directly," Donovan suggested. "Why don't they do that?"

"I don't believe they have enough physical form to make that happen," I told him. "Whatever they are, I don't believe they are from our physical plane. Wherever they came from must be very different from here."

Donovan looked at me for a very long time, as he unconsciously ran his fingers across his scaly scalp. I know I did something similar for a time when I was first transformed.

"Are there others out there like us," he asked me. "I would think there would be others."

"If there are others out there," I replied. "They have never made themselves known to me. The shadows have certainly never implied the existence of more like me."

Then I felt the call of my masters and I could see that Donovan felt it as well. We rose as one and returned to the mineshaft. Looking over my shoulder I saw the bare beginnings of the dawn been recognized that our Masters were being thoughtful. They could very well have given Donovan his first lesson in what happens when the light touches our skin.

I took Donovan to the shelf I had made in the mineshaft and we both easily climbed up into it. The shadows bundled on up with us and filled the shelf with their essence. With that odd ability they had, they kept us fixed in place and unable to move until they decided it was time.

We are going to keep an eye on you both, they told us. *Tomorrow you will take us with you, and we will tell you where you are going.*

"Where are we going?" I asked submissively.

We will tell you when the time comes, was the answer they gave.

"As you desire, masters," I replied.

Four

The shadows kept us in place for at least three days. We were both starving by that time, and while I had experienced this before, it was something entirely new for Donovan.

"It hurts," Donovan moaned. "I need to eat!"

You will eat when we say you may eat, the shadows told him sharply, *and not before. You are forbidden to eat until we tell you that you may.*

"I am sorry," he mumbled, clearly in pain. I remember my own time being trained in submission to their will, and resented that I was having to relearn it along with him.

I hurt as well, but I knew better than to say anything about it to the shadows. I didn't know what they might do to Donovan for his minor outburst, but torture was not something they were above.

The shadows went back to the floor of the mineshaft, and waited as we climbed down from the shelf. Instructing us to open our mouths, we did so, and the shadows flowed inside us. Donovan looked frightened, and again the shadows laughed.

"Where will you have us go," I asked them.

It is time that we moved, the shadows said. *Humans will be here soon with their construction equipment and light, and we must be away from that. There is another mine some distance from here, and we shall dwell there for a time.*

The shadows continued.

It is good that you brought us this new servant, as you would only have been able to carry one of us at a time.

With that, and because I had no personal possessions to speak of, we began our run to find this new mine of which the shadows were aware. I wondered how they knew, but decided it might have something to do with shadows knowing where to find other shadows. A small part of me wondered if there would be others like them where we were going.

The masters gave no answer to that.

We ran for most of the night and covered a great deal of ground. If the shadows had not been with us, we might have missed our destination.

I had no idea how long this particular mine had been abandoned, but the entrance was almost completely obscured by hardened mudslides and shrubbery. Ordering us to open our mouths once more they flowed out of us and slipped into a hole in the hard dirt.

Now go and feed if you can find prey before the dawn comes, the shadows instructed us, and they were gone.

Released from the absolute control of the past few days, I sniffed the air.

I could smell prey, probably not too far distant from where we stood. From the expression on Donovan's face, I could tell that he smelled prey as well. It took only a few more moments before he realized what it was that we smelled.

"I can't," he stammered. "I can't eat another human being!"

"Donovan," I told him warningly. "The shadows know what's here to eat, and you don't want them to get mad at you."

Eat, the shadows raged at us. *Do not disobey, or you will not like your punishment.*

And then we were running toward what must have been a hunting encampment. I could smell the beer and hear the snores of our unsuspecting prey.

"We have to feed on...humans?" Funny how easy it was to start differentiating species. I wondered if he realized what he'd said.

"For us, they are food," I said. "I know how hungry you are. Try to forget, and let your instincts take over."

The hunters were so intoxicated that they probably never knew what happened to them. As the element of surprise was not as necessary in this situation, I took my time. Both hunters were drunk off their asses, and probably nowhere near coordinated enough to put up a meaningful fight.

"Hello," I said to the hunter I had picked as my meal. "It's time for dinner."

My dinner guest opened his eyes blearily, trying to focus on my face. His brow wrinkled as he tried to make sense of what he saw, and I leaned forward so he could get a much better look at me.

I held his face in my hands and leaned in close with the last kiss he would ever feel. He screamed, slapping and punching at me ineffectually, trying to force me off of him. And that was when I began to feed.

His drunken terror was delicious.

Donovan was already feeding from his victim, not yet into playing with his food. I knew there would come a time when he would dawdle over his meal, but that time was not now. He would eventually revel in the terror he caused, just as I did.

I lingered over my meal. I didn't feed quickly at all, enjoying it immensely as the human tried to escape. My claws were latched into his clothing, so there was no chance of him wriggling free completely. Thus I allowed him to periodically move his mouth and nose away from mine, and I would give him a few moments of imagined hope before I dashed it again.

However, my play could only last so long. Relatively quickly, the human lost too much energy and began to fade. Using my personal form of a coup de grace, I clamped my mouth over his nose and mouth and sucked in the last of his body's energy as swiftly as I could. I watched his body collapse in upon itself much as a cigarette is consumed when one draws upon it as hard as possible.

Donovan had finished his meal a few moments earlier, and was now fingering the dust that was left behind. He ran a claw tip through a relatively dry pile of the stuff and watched as it tumbled over into the damp leaves.

"We don't really leave anything behind, do we?"

"Whenever possible, you want to finish what you start," I told him. "The last thing you need is a human remembering what happened, and telling enough people that someone finally believes him."

"I think I would have a hard time believing anyone who told me that something like us exists," he said. "It defies the laws of Nature."

"Oh, there are people out there who are actively searching us out in hopes of capturing one of us," I said. "They want to cage us and study us like lab rats. Never ever only snack from a human."

"Why did you not kill me," he asked me as we both got up and began our search for a place to hide from the light of day. "I know now how easy it would have been for you to do that."

"I really could not say," I admitted. "Normally I think I would have, perhaps it was your kindness or the fact that you didn't run screaming when you realized what was in that hole."

Donovan seemed to spend time absorbing what I told him. He appeared to have settled in quite nicely to the way whatever we were moved. I wondered if the shadows made slight changes to our brains as a way to make us more malleable, because I found walking on two legs uncomfortable and distasteful. They were able to control so much of me already; it didn't seem to be something out of the realm of possibility.

As I was very aware of the path the sun would take during the course of the day, I finally selected a rocky outcropping as our shelter. The small cave beneath it would be sufficient to conceal us both in the painful light that would soon be upon us.

"Why do we have to hide in the dark," he asked me as we started to settle in. "Can't we just find some other place to curl up?"

"Do you remember when you first found me and the sun's light landed on my leg?"

"I think so," he responded.

"If you look at my leg now," I told him. "You will see a wound there. That is a burn that came from just that small amount of light hitting my flesh. It felt as though I had been burned with fire, and it will take a week or two for it to heal completely. That is what any light other than moonlight will do to you as well."

Donovan lightly touched the area around the now healing burn. Despite the fact that it hurt like a son of a bitch, I allowed him to feel the damage that had been done by something as innocuous as a sunbeam. A moment later, he sat back.

"All of that came from sunlight? So any light, even a light bulb?"

"Yes, even a light bulb a small as a Christmas tree light will burn you to one degree or another. The level of the burn will vary, but you will be burned."

"That doesn't make sense," he protested. "Moonlight is simply reflected sunlight!"

"I didn't make the rules of what we are," I said. "Who knows why this all works the way it does? We are what we are and we're stuck this way."

"How long have you been this way," Donovan ventured after a few minutes. "Has it been a long time?"

"I had my first *meeting* with the shadows in 1958," I told him. "I have been their slave ever since then."

"How did you meet them? Did you make a habit of walking into old mines?"

"I fell into an old mineshaft," I replied. "I broke my leg on the way down and would have died down there. The shadows, seeing their opportunity, made me as I am now."

"Are there a lot of these shadows out there?"

"I only know about a relative few. Not all mines that I have been into since have had them," I explained. "I can't tell them apart. They may just be pieces of one original shadow, but I don't know. They choose whatever information they're going to share with me."

Conversation died, and turned into touching and exploring one another. I once again played with his dick, nibbling lightly on it as I sucked, and he writhed in response to that intimacy.

I teased the tip of his member with my tongue, exploring it, amazed that the masters had left us with this release. After his orgasm, Donovan moved to my crotch and engulfed it with his lips, nibbling and sucking at my clit until I could feel the pull of my orgasm in my knees and embraced it as it washed over my entire body, leaving me shaking, spent, and wildly satisfied, though still wanting more.

Eventually, we went to sleep, each with our own dreams.

I tended to dream about my family, but it had been so long since I had laid eyes on them that they had become abstract concepts in my mind. Flashes of memory: a flip of long red hair; a set of impossibly green eyes; a missing front tooth that seemed to belong to one of my little brothers.

My subconscious would often put those vague images together to create family gatherings and situations. In almost every single dream about my family, we were torn apart and I ended up falling down a dark tunnel that was both terrifying and soothing at the same time.

As always, I woke up as I hit the bottom of the tunnel. Donovan was already awake and looking at me.

"Are you okay? You were talking in your sleep," he told me. "It didn't sound good."

"It's nothing," I replied curtly. "We have to get going."

"Where do we have to go?"

"We have to find something to eat," I said. "The feeding never really ends."

"What about the shadows?"

"When they want us, we'll feel their call," I said bluntly.

The next several days and nights were a long succession of days spent sleeping through the day in whatever shelter we could find and then fucking and hunting during the nighttime hours. Most of our prey during this time were animals, although a few unlucky humans ended as piles of dust.

Once, as hungry as I was, I left a mother and child hiking in a local park alone. It would have been easy to take them, but this time, I could not bring myself to feed on them.

If you are reading this correctly, you will pick up on the fact that I have not been a saint. Hell, how can you be a saint when you do the kinds of things I must do in order to survive?

Donovan still had problems feeding, but could not prevent himself from doing so. One night, he tried to keep from feeding and ended up being attacked by a pack of five feral dogs who fed him anyway.

In the course of the altercation, he hit one so hard that it was knocked unconscious and he drank the other one down to dust on the spot. Their compatriots ran from the scene, yelping in terror.

I had been attacked by feral dogs before. They didn't seem to have the good sense that truly wild animals have when encountering something new and different. A wolf or a big cat rarely took the initiative to attack me, but feral dogs, on the other hand, just didn't seem to have the sense to stay away.

As feral dogs were dangerous to nearly anything in the areas they claimed as their territory, it didn't bother me in the least when I had the opportunity to thin out their numbers. When I was a kid, we lost a couple lambs to a roaming pack of the beasts, and I had never forgotten how hurt and angry that had made me feel.

Killing feral dogs made me happy, what can I say?

A DARKER SHADOW

I ran after the three who tried to escape and managed to cripple two of them, leaving a particularly agile young mutt as the sole surviving member of the formerly terrifying pack.

Donovan had been kind to the dog he'd knocked unconscious, compared to what I had done to the two I claimed for myself.

One had been thrown into a tree and while it was still alive, it was no longer able to walk. The second had two broken back legs, and it desperately tried to crawl away from me. My first meal would come from the one who'd been introduced to the tree, as it appeared it would die sooner than the one with broken legs.

While I didn't like feral dogs, I didn't see a reason to further torment them, so their endings were quick. When the one with the broken legs saw what was going on with its pack mate, it seemed to realize that it was probably going to be next in line at the buffet and actually tried to crawl away.

Of course, it was unsuccessful in its attempt at escape.

We didn't have much time left before we needed to return to our nest for the day once we had finished our hunt. It was the point during the summer months when there was far more sunlight than night, so our activities were fairly limited. I much preferred the winter months, when I could hunt and travel much farther in a single night's time.

Once the summer solstice did its thing, our time to rule the night would slowly increase until the winter solstice arrived and we once again began to lose our beloved darkness.

Donovan and I didn't really talk much. I could feel his anger at his situation, and I didn't blame him. I had had anger, too, when I had become what I was now. While he blamed me for his condition, I blamed myself for my stupidity in hiking without a companion.

We still had wild sex, as that helped to complete the release we sought when we fed, but it was almost a mechanical thing at this point. It was like the feeding had become foreplay and we had to bring things to a climax or lose our minds.

The shadows had probably done something to us when we had transported them the last time to make that necessary, if only to make sure we stayed together. Each time we had sex, or whatever you might call what we did, our minds seemed to move into harmony with one another.

Then, one night, we felt the pull of our masters and knew we had to start the trek back to where they hid underground. It was impossible to get lost when returning to them, as their demand shone like a beacon to us as we traveled in their direction.

We had to break through the small hole that the shadows had slipped through to enter the mineshaft, but were careful only to open it as far as absolutely necessary. Crawling over and around obstacles, we finally located our masters at the end of the furthest tunnel. There was an odd lumpy, rocky thing near where they rested.

"You called?"

You must go to another nest a great distance from here and bring back the one who nests there, they told us. *Return as quickly as you are able, or there will be consequences.*

"I am only able to move so fast, my masters," I replied. "But I will move as quickly as I am able."

The shadows laughed and moved.

I could not help but scream as the shadows engulfed me, and heard Donovan scream as well. I could not figure out what I may have done to make them angry, but I could feel it as my body seemed to start to melt into some other shape.

Oh please, god, not the worm again! Nonono! Ipromiseillbegood! Pleasepleaseplease...

And then, as my body twisted and writhed in agony, I lost consciousness.

Five

When I woke up, I knew something was very different. I was afraid to open my eyes, but the shadows knew I was awake and would not let me just lay there.

It is time for you to travel, so awaken and run!

I opened my eyes and the first thing I saw was that we had been somehow moved outside of the mine's entrance. I was not sure how the shadows might have accomplished that, but knew better than to ask.

Looking over to my left, I saw what must have been Donovan in front of me, but I would not have known it was him if I had not experienced the same thing he had.

It seemed I could just barely pick up on what he was thinking, as wildly unlikely as that might seem. I wondered what the shadows had done this time.

He looked something like a dog, but much more compact. In fact, he was about the height of a good-sized German Shepherd.

I felt a mixture of anger and embarrassment coming from him and tried to send back the message that he should school his thoughts. I saw him look startled and knew that he'd picked up on what I was trying to tell him.

The black eyes and scaly skin were the same, of course. Donovan's long dog's head had a slightly larger than normal mouth, and when he opened it, I saw the same kind of sharp teeth it had contained in its former incarnation. I was instantly reminded of the hellhounds in the forbidden comic books I had read without my parents' knowledge.

Looking down, I saw that I was similarly equipped. I tried to speak, but only an odd whistling sound emerged from my throat. So they had decided that I should be punished for my unintended insolence, I decided. It was not as though they needed me to speak aloud to know what I wanted to say. Dog lips aren't designed for speech, after all, which I am certain my masters knew well.

But why punish Donovan as well?

You are now able to run very quickly, the shadows told me. *Start running now, and you may make a good distance before the sun rises again. We have given you your destination already. We have placed it in your mind.*

Unable to stop myself, I whined my unhappiness. I flinched, fully expecting a reprimand. I was shocked when none came. And then came another surprise.

You are still able to communicate with one another, but we think that you have had entirely too much of an opportunity to speak together and not focus on your tasks. Perhaps you need a reminder of what is important and what is not.

So that is what that had been all about. Apparently the two of us now shared a weak combination of telepathy and empathy, but not enough of either to have a real conversation.

Wishing we had the time to work out the parameters of our new method of communication, it appeared as though that would not be possible. I didn't want to aggravate the shadows further, as they had not been as cruel as it might have been.

A DARKER SHADOW

Donovan and I left the area at a dead run, impelled by the orders we had received, covering the ground at an astonishing rate of speed. I could not help shrilling a challenge to the quarter moon that hung low on the horizon, and wondered what else the shadows had done to me.

Something was very, very wrong, but I was not able to put a name to it. Not yet, anyway.

I hated that I was only able to communicate with Donovan through strong emotions and thoughts, and it would have been so very much better if we had been allowed to speak. The knowledge of our destination was held fast in my brain and we homed in on it, only deviating from our course in order to find daily shelter.

Over the course of several days, and several times fucking one another, we began to find it easier to communicate. With this transformation, the masters had given me something like a vagina, and Donovan would climb atop me, shoving his dick inside me and locking his jaws on the back of my neck to hold me in place while he rode me to orgasm again and again.

Sometimes it even seemed as though we began doing things in unison. If I had really paid attention to it, I have noticed what was going on and become more concerned.

I really should have been paying more attention, but I wasn't.

It had become apparent that our journey would take us very close to human habitation and I was not sure how we would manage to make our way through them. I decided that our best bet would be to find a rundown area, as places such as that often had fewer devices around that offered artificial light that would burn us as surely as the sun's light would.

I will admit that it also crossed my mind that we would find food in such an area, as heavily rundown neighborhoods seem to be magnets for all sorts of unsavory characters and their bad behavior.

If I didn't have to eat someone who was only minding their own business, why not? Donovan apparently picked up the gist of what I was thinking and I felt his agreement in my own mind.

Slinking through the streets, where our outlines but not our actual characteristics could be seen, we sought out good candidates for a filling meal.

We turned our attention to one house in particular where the stench of an unwashed body filled the air, and I was not surprised when a figure stumbled out of an open door and lurched into the street. If we had had stomachs, they would have been rumbling with hunger.

It was all we could do to keep from jumping the human immediately and beginning to feed. Donovan slipped around to one side of the human, while I waited on the near side. We waited.

"Here, doggie," the human mumbled as he noticed us on the dark street. One hand was stretched out in welcome, while his other hand fumbled behind his back. I was fairly certain that there was something nasty being concealed back there and hoped that Donovan saw it as well. "C'mere, doggie. I have something for you."

Oh yes, I am sure you do.

Donovan began to move around toward the back of the human, who was forced to turn in order to keep his hand from being seen. He obviously had not yet seen what we really looked like. Or perhaps he thought he was seeing things anyway. Either way, his caution would not save him.

"It's almost like you know what I am thinking," he muttered to himself, as there would be no reason he'd actually speak to a dog and expect it to understand him.

The fool.

At the same instant, and without even thinking about it, we both leaped in, knocking the human to the ground. He would have screamed, but I had already clamped my mouth over his nose and mouth, smothering the sound. Donovan stood guard as I sucked down the human's life, knowing that I would help him to feed once I was finished with my own feast. It was important to keep guard while I fed.

Donovan's meal was not long in coming, as another human wobbled out of the same doorway.

"Rick? Fuck man, where'd you go?"

We didn't give this one the chance to make it to the sidewalk, and moved quickly to intercept him. So few of the humans know when to run.

Donovan was on the human faster than the human eye could register, and gulping his life essence. The wonderful feeling of the energy as it entered my body brought up that feeling of unquenched desire and I knew I would have to deal with it.

Once his meal had been reduced to dust, we both stood and shook ourselves as though to knock the dust loose from our hides. Then we entered the house.

I could easily smell that humans had recently been in the house, but I didn't pick up the aroma of any current residents. I did, however, pick up the smell of death and rot. As I looked at Donovan, it was clear that he also could sense it.

I picked my way upstairs and looked into the smoke and filth-stained rooms that contained urine-soaked mattresses and the remains of intravenous drug kits.

In one of the rooms, I found the remains of a mostly decomposed human. Most of the flesh on the body had rotted away or had been eaten by flies and beetles, but there was enough of the chest and hair remaining to see that it had once been a woman with long straw-colored hair. There was no evidence to show what had killed her, and as she could not feed either of me, she was of no importance.

How had the humans been able to stay where a rotting body stunk up the air? It made no sense to me.

Going back downstairs and finding the kitchen, I discovered a door that looked as though it might lead down into a basement. Fortunately, it was ajar, so I pushed it the rest of the way open and went down into the blissfully dark and cool cellar.

It had apparently already been ransacked by the squatters, but I found some ratty old clothing piled in a corner and curled up on that for the day. It had been a long time since I had had a soft bed of any sort on which to sleep, and it was a wonderful place where we could fuck again.

When we were through, Donovan and I lay very close together, as we had been doing since being placed in this form. I suddenly realized that it was very difficult to think of myself as an individual, and wondered if it was Donovan or me who was having that thought.

I was terrified of what the next night would bring. How much longer would it be before I was no longer Bridget and he was no longer Donovan? Bits and pieces of who I was were being whittled away, and it seemed there was nothing I could do to keep it from happening.

And would we miss ourselves as a result?

I got up and sniffed the air, I could make out the scent of humans nearby. They may have found the house empty except for the corpse upstairs, and decided to make use of the premises.

I seemed to hear something laughing somewhere, but I didn't understand where the laughter came from. I only knew that bothered me. The shrillness hurt my ears and I shook my head unhappily.

I licked the day's dust from my head and body, suddenly desiring to be clean. The humans upstairs didn't appear to be moving around much, so I probably had a little time before I could have something to eat.

Something pushed up against my mind, like a butterfly attempting to escape a cocoon. It wriggled and itched and I did my best to ignore it, as I had work to do in order to make the Masters pleased. I liked it when the Masters were pleased.

After making quick work of the humans I left the house happy and sated, and the sounds of my eight paws echoed on the pavement as I ran.

As I continued to run, I felt pleasure in knowing that the Masters would be happy. The itching started again and I tried once again to ignore it. I tried to distract myself by looking at the ground I covered, but the itching seemed to turn into a voice. I wondered if it was the Masters speaking to me.

The fog lifted a little bit.

I need to be myself, I told myself, as I worked to wrench my brain free from Donovan's. The Masters had done an excellent job of starting the process of turning us into an obedient unit.

I felt it as my brain worked to rejoin Donovan's, and fought against it as hard as I could.

It was as though each of our brains were opposing hands and fingers from one body and each sought the grasp of the other to become comfortable once again. Insert Tab A into Slot B.

Both Donovan and I stumbled and came to a halt as I forced the wedge as far as I could between our brains. It was not a perfect split, but for now anyway we were not a single unit.

Hard to think, I thought at him as hard as I could. He shook his head as if to clear it. It was the first individual thought I had had in a long since they had wrought this new change upon us.

Yes, was all he seemed to be able to manage.

Shadows did this, I pressed further. I saw the fear enter his eyes and knew that he'd caught at least part of it.

Losing myself, he thought. *Scared*.

I wondered how much of Donovan was left in there now. I only knew about myself for sure.

I felt the shadows notice what was going on and there was a surge...

At the masters' command, we fucked one another over and over again, each joining blending our minds even further. My love for the masters surged within me as my teeth grasped the nape of my neck in my teeth and I shoved my dick over and over again into my tight, willing cunt. Only when my masters were happy could I be happy.

It was the natural order of things.

The fog blanketed my mind again and I started running. I had to get to my destination soon, or the Masters would be angry again and punish me. I should not make them mad. It was wrong of me to make the Masters mad.

A DARKER SHADOW

I managed to break through a few times during the run to our destination, but it was more and more difficult each time to force myself through. It was just so much easier to let myself fall back into the small hive mind that Donovan and I had, no thanks to the shadows.

I didn't want to lose myself completely, but didn't know how long it would be until I was no longer myself.

And then I was running again, my eight feet striking the ground tirelessly in a long lope. My destination was near and the Masters would be happy with me. My only goal in my existence was to make them happy and I would not fail them this time.

Don't miss out!

Visit the website below and you can sign up to receive emails whenever Jacqui Callen publishes a new book. There's no charge and no obligation.

https://books2read.com/r/B-A-VGNF-LQTQ

BOOKS 2 READ

Connecting independent readers to independent writers.